Wombat Went A' Walking

A Lothian Children's Book

Published in Australia and New Zealand in 2011
by Hachette Australia
Level 17, 207 Kent Street, Sydney NSW 2000
www.hachettechildrens.com.au

12

National Library of Australia
Cataloguing-in-Publication data

Lachlan Creagh.
Wombat went a' walking / Lachlan Creagh.

978 0 7344 1223 2 (hbk.)
978 0 7344 1264 5 (pbk.)

For pre-school age.
Wombat went a' walking-Juvenile fiction.

A823.4

Designed by Jo Hunt
Colour reproduction by Splitting Image
Printed in China by Toppan Leefung

Wombat Went A' Walking

LOTHIAN
Children's Books

Illustrated by

Lachlan Creagh

Wombat went a' **walking** and stopped to cool his feet,
He saw a giant turtle **climb** out of the creek.
"Hey, lazybones, there's no time to rest.

I'm going to a **dance**, will you be my guest?"

First on their journey, they passed a billabong,

They saw a magpie **dancing**, all on her own.

"We're going to a place where we can make a fuss.

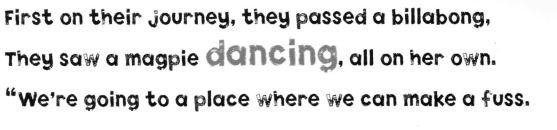

Here's a **great** idea - why not follow us?"

They **Shimmied** **Up** and **Over** a big black rock,

And woke a goanna who was sleeping like a log.

He opened one eye

and gave a wicked hiss.

But he smiled when he saw them jive and twist.

High in a gumtree a kookaburra sat,

With a **belly** full of lunch he was feeling very **fat**.

"I need some exercise, so can I come along?"

Goanna said, "**yes**, if you'll sing us all a song."

A red kangaroo came **hopping** on by,

"You sure can **dance**, but I'll bet you can't **JUMP** high!"

"You've got it wrong!" said magpie, as they bounced and bopped about.

So roo leaped even higher with a holler and a shout.

At the bottom of a gully, a croc was thumping in the muck,

"I want to come **dancing**, but I think I'm stuck."

So they all linked up like a **rocking, rolling** train.

And they **pulled**, and they **pulled**, till he was free again.

Running through the scrub a crazy emu **dashed**,

She was moving so fast that they nearly all **crashed**,

"I'd really like to party but first I have to know.

Can you teach me to boogie **nice** and **slow**?"

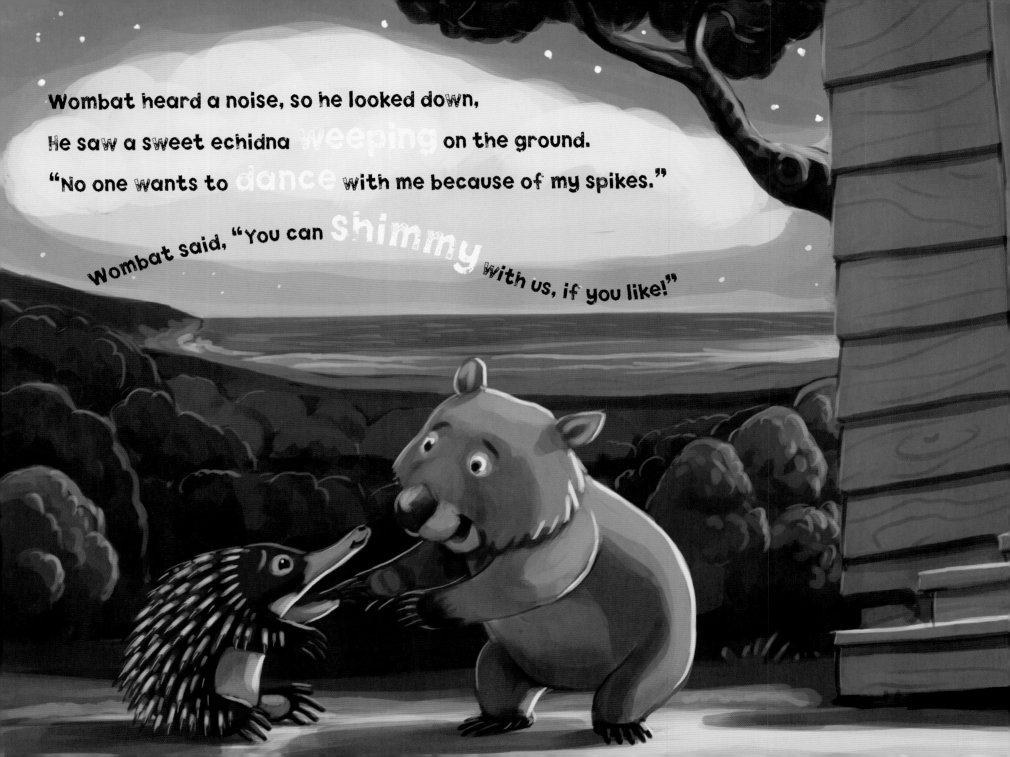

Wombat heard a noise, so he looked down,

He saw a sweet echidna weeping on the ground.

"No one wants to dance with me because of my spikes."

Wombat said, "You can shimmy with us, if you like!"

They danced all evening and all through the night,

Then they sat on the beach till morning light.

Then it was time to go their separate ways,

So they all said, "Let's meet again and **dance** another day!"

"Wake up, lazybones -
we're feeling so **alive!**

"It's time to spring and leap about - time to have a jive."

Wombat's **woken** up,

so let's go back to the start.

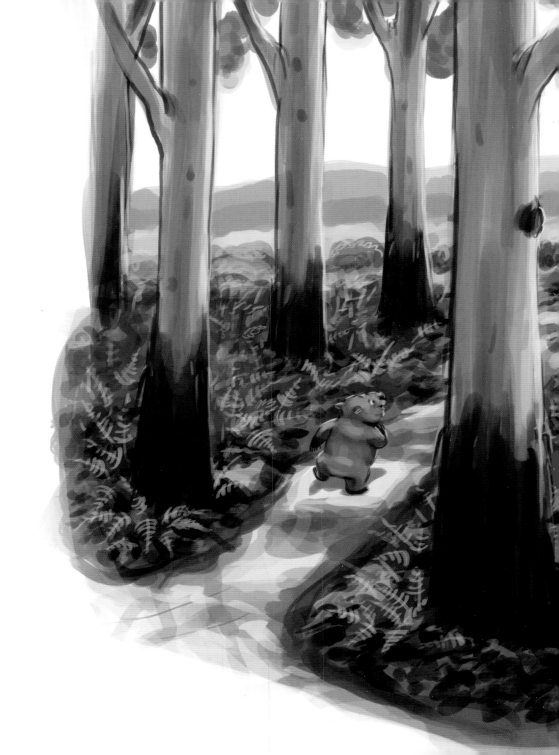

"Wake up, lazybones -
we're feeling so alive!

So they all said,

"Let's meet again and **dance** another day!"

Then it was time to go
their separate ways,